A.J. sighed. Hallow good thing to look f

had said he needed

The bus driver had yelled at him that morning.
Mrs. Todd had assigned another book report.
And he had another spelling test on Friday.

Why couldn't grown-ups just leave him
alone? They were always ordering him around,
getting on him about something or other.
Adults sure knew how to mess up his life!

Be sure to read all the books in the Golden Rule Duo series:

And the Winner Is . . .
Trick 'N' Trouble

TRiCK 'N' TROUBLE

by Janet Holm McHenry

Illustrated by Donna Kae Nelson

Chariot Books™
A Division of Cook Communications

Chariot Books™ is an imprint of David C. Cook Publishing Co.
David C. Cook Publishing Co., Elgin, Illinois 60120
David C. Cook Publishing Co., Weston, Ontario
Nova Distribution Ltd., Eastbourne, England

TRICK 'N' TROUBLE
© 1994 by Janet Holm McHenry for text and Donna Kae Nelson
for illustrations

Scripture quotations are from the *Holy Bible, New International
Version,* © 1973, 1978, 1984, International Bible Society. Used by
permission of Zondervan Bible Publishers.

Designed by Larry Taylor
First Printing, 1994
Printed in the United States of America
98 97 96 95 94 5 4 3 2 1

Library of Congress Cataloging-in-Publication Data
McHenry, Janet Holm.
Trick 'n' Trouble / by Janet Holm McHenry.
P.   cm. — (The Golden Rule Duo)
Summary: Upset with the adults in his life, A.J. decides to join his friends in playing
a Halloween trick on their fourth grade teacher—despite the objections of his twin
sister, Emily.
ISBN 0-7814-0171-2
[1. Twins—Fiction. 2. Brothers and sisters—Fiction. 3. Schools—Fiction. 4.
Christian life—Fiction. 5. Halloween—Fiction.] I. Title. II. Title: Trick and trouble
III. Series: McHenry, Janet Holm. Golden Rule Duo.
PZ7.M478627Tr 1994
[Fic]—dc20   94-6635   CIP   AC

Do to others
as you would have them
do to you.
Luke 6:31

Contents

Failing the Test

A.J. couldn't believe his spelling test. A big red F was written on the top. Mrs. Todd must have made a mistake. He had never gotten an F in his life! Until now, that is, in the fourth grade.

"Mrs. Todd," he said, waving his hand.

Mrs. Todd, the new, young teacher, was handing out weekly progress reports. With the report was all the work the students had done the week before.

"Mr. Roberts," Mrs. Todd replied, tripping over a backpack sticking out from underneath a desk.

"I think you may have made a mistake here," said A.J. "I only missed six."

Mrs. Todd peered through her eyeglasses, balancing the pile of reports on her hip.

"No, that's correct," said Mrs. Todd. "You missed six out of twelve, A.J. That means you only got half right. Half is only fifty percent. That's not a passing grade."

"But I only missed six on my math test and I got an A on it," he argued.

"Yes, Anthony," she said. "But there were 100 questions on that test. You'll learn more about percentages as the year goes on. Just study your spelling harder next time."

Anthony Jacob Roberts turned three shades of red, almost matching his auburn hair and '49ers shirt. He looked across the room where his twin sister, Emily, was sitting. There she was, turned around, showing off what was probably another perfect progress report.

Emily noticed A.J. looking at her. *Whatja get?* she mouthed, swinging her strawberry-blonde ponytail back and forth.

He stuck out his tongue. Just what he needed, to be in the same class—again—with his smart aleck sister.

I'm going to be grounded for sure, he thought. No friends, no TV, maybe even no soccer. And with the tournament coming this weekend!

"Okay," announced Mrs. Todd, "there's the bell. Remember to come tomorrow with ideas for a Halloween party. If I've checked your homework book, you may go."

Anthony crumpled up his spelling test, stuffed it into the bottom of his backpack, and was out the door all in one motion.

"Halloween," he mumbled under his breath.

That was about the only good thing to look forward to this week. Dad had said A.J. needed to rake leaves after school. The bus driver had yelled at him that morning. Mrs. Todd had assigned another book report. And he had another spelling test on Friday.

Why couldn't grown-ups just leave him alone? They were always ordering him around, getting on him about something or other. Adults sure knew how to mess up his life!

Looking
for Sympathy

A.J. soon found out that he was not alone. His best buddy, Zak the Short, also bombed the spelling test. So did Tyler. So did Mike.

Before school on Tuesday, the four boys sat on the edge of the blacktop playground behind Pine Tree Elementary. They were throwing pebbles at a large pinecone about ten feet away.

"I'm grounded from my Nintendo," said Zak.

"I'm grounded from Nintendo and TV," said Tyler.

"I'm grounded from Nintendo, TV, and my Walkman," said Mike.

A.J. huffed and threw a larger rock at the pinecone. He sent it spinning.

CHAPTER TWO

"You think that's bad," he said. "I'm grounded from life, forever doomed to study spelling words twenty-four hours a day."

Zak shook his head and threw an even larger rock. "That's bad. Grounded from life."

"Boys! Boys!"

The boys froze, and slowly turned their heads. It was Mr. Lightfoot, the principal. Mr. Lightfoot always meant business.

The tall man in a dark suit stood over them. His figure was outlined by the sun which was rising above the pine trees around the school.

"No throwing rocks, boys," he said. "You know the rules."

"Yes, sir," they all chimed, rising slowly and brushing pine needles from their jeans.

"Find something better to do," Mr. Lightfoot chided.

The four boys nodded and walked to another corner of the playground.

"That's the trouble around here," said A.J.

"What?" said Zak.

"Too many adults making too many rules about too many things," replied A.J.

"Yeah," said Mike. "They treat us like little kids."

"Yeah," said Tyler. "I had to go to bed at eight last night."

"I had to do the dishes and go to bed at eight," said Zak.

"I had to do the dishes, take out the trash, and go to bed at eight," said Mike.

"You think that's bad," said A.J. "I had to do all of that and be grounded from life."

The other boys just shook their heads. Then they remembered that Halloween was coming. Tyler said his mom wanted him to wear his bear costume again. The other boys teased him, even after the whistle blew for lineup time. Nobody in the fourth grade wore a bear costume for Halloween! Nobody!

Adults.

Planning the Party 3

Mrs. Todd was reading announcements from the *Pine Tree Elementary Daily News*. Friday there would be a school-wide parade with all the kids in Halloween costumes.

"What about a party?" asked Annie Rose.

"Well, I guess now is as good a time as any to talk about it," said Mrs. Todd.

"First I need to tell you that I'm not crazy about Halloween," she said. "It has to do with my faith. I can't explain it, because I'm your teacher. I'm not supposed to talk about those things."

"Does that mean we won't have a party?" asked Tyler. The class grumbled.

"No," said Mrs. Todd. "I know it's important

to you. We'll have a party. I would just prefer you forget the scary part of Halloween. It's the witches and ghosts that I don't like."

Everyone was quiet for a moment. No one knew what to say, not even Zak, which was unusual. They had never heard a teacher say anything like that before.

"My mom could make cupcakes," said Annie Rose quietly.

"I could bring a punch," said Tyler, grinning and hitting his left palm with his right fist.

"We could bring popcorn," said Emily. "We've got LOTS of popcorn. You wouldn't believe this bag of popcorn we've got. It's as big as . . ."

"Thank you, Emily," said Mrs. Todd. "That would be great. Well, people, it sounds like we're going to have a party Friday."

"Trick or treat," said A.J., tapping his fingers.

"Well, treats anyway," said Mrs. Todd. "Hopefully no tricks."

Pulling the Party

In class on Wednesday morning, A.J. stared out into space. That was normal. It was writing project time. A.J. hated writing.

He looked over at Emily. She was writing like crazy. Behind her Annie Rose was too.

BEEP! BEEP! BEEP! BEEP!

Whew! Fire drill!

"Line up and file out quickly, people!" Mrs. Todd demanded.

Noisily the students filed down the hill to their spot on the playground. Fire drills were a normal part of school. A.J. liked them, especially when they came during writing time.

But just as he found his spot in line, a city

fire engine pulled into the parking lot next to the playground! And then another behind it!

"Zak!" A.J. yelled, tugging his friend's shirt. "Look! It's the real thing!"

Other students began yelling and jumping and pointing.

Soon there were two sheriffs' cars, an ambu-ance, and a half dozen cars with volunteer fire fighters racing from them. All of them seemed to come within seconds, and they ran toward the office on the first level.

Mr. Lightfoot and his secretary, Mrs. Sweat, came out the front door. They nodded, then Mr. Lightfoot walked over to the playground and talked with the teachers, one by one.

"Students!" said Mrs. Todd. "Students, please!"

The thirty chattering mouths finally slowed to a quiet hum.

"We've just been told it's a false alarm," said Mrs. Todd. "Some student pulled it on the second level. You can cause a lot of trouble when you do something like this.

"Mr. Lightfoot says that if the culprit doesn't confess, we won't have a Halloween parade on Friday. And we teachers agree there will be no parties, either."

Zak elbowed A.J. in the ribs. "That's a bunch of junk," he whispered. "One person does something wrong, and we all have to pay for it?"

"Yeah," said A.J. "Adults! They sure take it out on us kids, don't they?"

"That's no way to treat us," said Zak.

A.J. didn't answer. He was staring into space. He couldn't do something about all the adults in his life, but he could get back at one of them.

Zak waved his hands in front of A.J.'s eyes.

"I just got a great idea," A.J. said. "An A.J. original!"

"What?" asked Zak.

"If Mrs. Todd is going to treat us this way, we could treat her, too. We can treat her to a trick!"

Zak smiled.

A.J. continued. "I think it's time for a trick on old Teacher Todd. What do you think?"

"Cool," said Zak.

"Double cool," said A.J.

"Triple cool," said Zak.

"It's a triple dip cool then," said A.J. "We'll play a trick on Teacher Todd Friday. Tell the guys about it. We'll start planning it at lunch."

Planning the Trick

A.J., wait up!" Emily scooted around some other students to slip in beside her brother. It wasn't easy to catch him in the crowded cafeteria.

"This is a boys' table, Emmo," said A.J., biting into his peanut butter and jelly sandwich. He looked around to make sure Zak and company didn't see him with his sister, but they were at the other end of the table.

"I know," she replied, pulling out her identical sandwich. "But A.J., wasn't Mrs. Todd amazing?"

"Amazingly what?" A.J. asked.

"Amazingly Christian," said Emily. "At least I think she's a Christian now. You know, from what she said about Halloween and her faith and all."

"All she said, Emmo," said A.J., "was that she didn't like witches and stuff. She didn't say she was a Christian."

"I know, Dummo," said Emily. "But that's the same kind of stuff Mom and Dad talk about. You know they don't like Halloween either . . . and they're Christians."

"Yeah, so?" said A.J.

"Oh, you're just still mad about that spelling grade," said Emily. "And being grounded from . . ."

"From life," finished A.J.

"That's not what Mom and Dad said and you know it," said Emily. "You just have to miss out on a few things until your spelling grade gets better."

A.J. stuffed the entire second half of his sandwich in his mouth, all at once.

"That could be life," he mumbled, crumbs falling into his lap. "And it's Mrs. Todd's fault."

CHAPTER FIVE

Emily pointed a carrot stick at him. "It's not her fault, A.J., and you know it. You're the one who didn't study. It's your grade, not hers."

A.J. grabbed the carrot and bit off the end.

"Well, where did she get those spelling words anyway?" he asked. "I've never had to study spelling before in my life."

Emily stole one of A.J.'s nacho chips. "We're

in the fourth grade now, A.J. These words are harder; they're from our novels. You know that! We're just doing harder stuff this year."

A.J. frowned at her. "Whose side are you on—mine or Mrs. Toad's?"

"That's a mean thing to say," Emily said. "I'm just trying to help. I heard you might be playing a trick on Mrs. Todd, and I hoped it wasn't true."

"Trick or treat," said A.J. with a smile. "It's the week for that, you know."

"I know," said Emily. "That's what I was worried about. I really like Mrs. Todd. I think she's neat."

"I just want to have some fun," said A.J.

"Yeah," said Emily, "but don't do it at the expense of other people."

"Oh, don't worry," said A.J., scrunching his paper lunch bag. "We're sparing no expense. You'll see."

Chewing the Fat

Swish! Two points! A.J. sunk his lunch bag in the corner garbage can. Not a bad shot from where he sat. It might even have been three points.

"Anthony Roberts!"

Caught again! It was the duty aide.

A.J. turned around, holding his hands out in a question.

"That's detention time for you, young man," she said. "You know this is not a gymnasium. Go sit on the detention bench outside."

Outside, A.J. dragged his feet and sat sadly down on the bench. Adults! Why didn't they just leave him alone?

First the F, then being grounded, and now

detention. And to top it all off, they still didn't know if they'd get to have their party on Friday. The culprit hadn't confessed yet.

Adults.

"Hey, A.J., what's up?" It was Zak and company.

He and Mike and Tyler all sat down with A.J. on the bench.

"We decided we'd go for a bucket and join you," Zak said.

"Yeah," said Mike. "We thought it'd be a good time to plan the Teacher Toad trick."

"Good thinking, guys," said A.J. "So . . . any ideas?"

The four swung their feet for a few moments, looking up into the mellowing October sunlight.

"Worms are good," said Zak.

"Yup, worms are good," said Mike, "or cold spaghetti."

"Nah, not cold spaghetti," said Tyler. "That's little kids' stuff. We did that in the first grade."

"Okay, then," said A.J., "it's worms."

"How about a snake?" asked Zak. "I saw a dead one in the road by my house this morning."

"I saw a dead cat in the ditch this morning," said Mike.

"Yeah?" said Tyler. "A dead cat would be great for a Halloween trick!"

"Okay, then," said A.J., "it's a dead cat."

"I don't know," said Zak. "Mrs. Todd's brother is the science teacher at the high school. He uses dead cats for experiments. I bet she sees dead cats in his freezer all the time."

"Okay, then," said A.J., "it's the snake."

"I don't know," said Zak. "That snake I saw might have been a fan belt. Aren't all the snakes hibernating now?"

"Okay, then," said A.J., "we need to think of something we know she doesn't like."

"Like late homework?" joked Zak, elbowing A.J. in the ribs.

A.J. elbowed him back, and like a set of

dominoes, the three boys fell off the bench.

"Hey!" yelled Mike.

"Talk about tricks!" yelled Tyler.

Breeeeeet!

All four boys instantly knew what that sound was—the dreaded whistle of Ms. Morebucket. They stood to attention. No one messed with Ms. Morebucket.

"Now you've done it," whispered Mike.

"You four troublemakers march to the office!" commanded Ms. Morebucket. "I'm writing you up!"

All four marched to the office.

A.J. took the seat next to Mr. Lightfoot's door.

What is it with adults? he thought. *They're all on my case. Mrs. Todd. Mom and Dad. The duty aides. I don't think there's one adult in the world I can . . .*

A.J. thought for a moment. There was an adult he liked once. Last year when he and Emily went to summer camp, there was that counselor. Beef.

A.J. laughed inside.

What a crazy name—Beef! But it sure fit him. He must have been six foot four and 250 pounds! He was a tackle for the University of California.

Wow . . . a college football player. That's

what A.J. wanted to be some day. Maybe next year he could join Pop Warner, the football team for kids. Nah, Mom'd never let him. She'd worry about him getting hurt.

I guess some adults are okay, A.J. thought. *Beef was so cool. I used to be really shy talking about God stuff until I met Beef. He'd talk all day about how Jesus Christ changed his life. I might never have asked the Lord into my life if it weren't for Beef.*

Okay, God. So Beef was cool. And You're cool. And sometimes Mom and Dad are a little bit cool. But this Mrs. Todd, I don't know, God. She's been pretty hard on me.

"Anthony!"

A.J. looked up. It was Mrs. Sweat, the school secretary.

"Mr. Lightfoot will see you now."

Casting the Spell

Five minutes later A.J. slumped out of Mr. Lightfoot's office.

It wasn't bad. There in his office, Mr. Lightfoot was calm and quiet—not like out on the playground. And not mean like A.J. had expected.

Mr. Lightfoot believed A.J.'s story and let the other boys go.

"You can hurt someone when you're not thinking about what you're doing," he had said. "Be more careful from now on."

Outside, the three other boys circled around A.J.

"I don't smell dead meat," said Zak. "You okay?"

A.J. nodded.

Mike put one arm around his right shoulder; Tyler joined him on the other side.

"You're triple dip cool," said Mike.

"Yeah," said Tyler, "to take the blame for that. You're a real bud."

"So," said Zak, forming a huddle, "we've got the triple dip answer to this teacher trick question."

A.J. started to speak, but Zak kept talking.

"Remember how Mrs. Toad gave that boring speech about how she doesn't like witches and stuff?"

"Yeah . . ." said A.J.

"Well, we thought the perfect trick would be to dress like witches," said Mike.

"That's it?" asked A.J., throwing his hands up in the air. "That's the whole thing?"

"Not quite," said Tyler. "The best part is that we . . ."

"We," interrupted Zak, "each wear a sign that

says Mrs. Toad on the back."

"Oh, real good," said A.J. "So we all get into trouble, and I land right back in Mr. Lightfoot's office."

"No," said Mike, "not the way we've got it planned."

"Yeah," said Tyler. "You see, we all wear a mask. And lots of others will have masks, too. And we'll have everyone in the class switch seats. She'll never know who's who."

A.J. was quiet for a moment. He tapped his finger on his cheek. Slowly a smile started at the corners of his mouth, and spread widely until his eyes were fully lit like a fire. It wasn't like a fire that warmed, though. It was like a fire that could burn and destroy.

"Guys," he said, "you have created the perfect trick. But listen, let's keep this to ourselves. And especially don't tell Emily."

"Don't tell Emily what?"

The four boys froze. They hadn't noticed

that Emily and several of her friends had walked up as they were talking.

"I said, don't tell Emily what?" she repeated.

"Uh, uh, uh," said A.J., "we're uh, uh, going to have a surprise party for you, Emmo."

"Oh, right," said Emily, her hands on her hips. "Like I believe that! I think you guys were talking about this teacher trick thing."

"Us?" said Zak. "You mean innocent us?"

"Yeah, you," said Emily, "and you're certainly not innocent. I'd definitely say you're up to something."

"Up, down, around," chanted A.J.

"Lost or found," added Zak.

"In a costume," continued Mike.

"Riding a broom," finished Tyler.

"Thanks for the insult, guys," said Emily. "But just look out. I'm going to be watching you."

Spelling the Cast

Thursday morning A.J. doodled in his journal. He was supposed to be writing. Boy, he hated writing. He looked at Zak across from him in his group. Wait a minute! He was writing like crazy! And Zak hated writing too!

Zak looked up for a moment then tore a sheet of paper out of his journal. He wrote something on it, and passed it to A.J. It said:

> *How do you spell Mike's last name? And Tyler's?*

A.J. wrote back:

> *Duh. I flunked spelling. What are you doing?*

Zak wrote back:

Tell you later.

A.J. shook his head. Zak was a funny guy—always doing something different. That was why he liked him a lot. But sometimes that was why he didn't like him. Too bad Zak didn't know Jesus like A.J. did. Maybe someday . . .

The school day dragged. Mrs. Todd loaded on the work. And she wasn't budging: No party unless the fire alarm culprit confessed.

In the bus line after school, the four boys stood together.

"Hey, why did you need those names in class?" A.J. asked Zak.

"I'm writing a letter about Mrs. Toad," said Zak. "And I'm going to send it to the head guy down at the head office . . . what do they call it?"

"The district office?" said A.J.

"Yeah," said Zak. "I'm writing a letter about Mrs. Toad and her talking about her religion in our class and not letting us wear the costumes we want and about how she grades unfairly and is cancelling our party. Maybe we can get rid of her for good!"

"What!" croaked A.J. "She didn't really talk about her religion, you know. She just said she doesn't like witches."

"So? It's the best way," said Zak. "She'll be out of here in no time . . . especially with our parents' names on it."

"What!" croaked A.J. again. "Our parents' names? How will you get their names on it?"

"Just sign 'em," said Zak. "That's why I needed the spellings. I could spell Roberts, but I didn't know the others. By the way, I got them from brainchild Brandon."

"Zak," said A.J., "you can't do that! Someone could find out. Someone could get in trouble— like you and me!"

"You're just chicken," said Zak. "You'll go for the little trick or treat thing, but you die on me when I have a good idea."

As the other guys filed into the bus, A.J. held

back a moment, pulling Zak aside.

"I'm not quitting on you, Zak," said A.J., "but maybe this is just going too far."

"Hey, glad you're with me," said Zak, pulling away. "Just think, we could be rid of Mrs. Toad."

No more Mrs. Toa . . . Todd? A.J. thought as he dragged his feet up the bus steps. No more F's on spelling tests? No more writing time? That sounded good, but . . .

God, this is all happening too fast! What am I supposed to do now?

37

Blowing the Disguise

Things were wild Friday from the first bell. It started when Mrs. Todd thought she had a new student. "She" turned out to be Riley dressed in his sister's cheerleader outfit. He got sent home.

Jason dressed like a hockey player and roller-bladed to school. He was sent home too.

Then "Mary Ann" sneezed during a science experiment, and her doctor's mask fell down. It turned out she was not Mary Ann, but Crystal from Mr. Moore's fourth-grade class.

All morning long there was buzzing and note passing. As the boys had planned, one of the notes read, "Sit in the wrong seat after lunch."

The students still didn't know if they would

get their parade and party, so they were making the most of their time in their costumes.

When the lunch bell rang, Mrs. Todd reminded the class that there would be no party or parade that afternoon if the fire alarm puller did not confess. And the students would have to take off their costumes.

On the way out of class, A.J. felt a hand slam on his shoulder.

"Trick time!" It was Zak, with Tyler and Mike beside him.

In the boys' bathroom, things were crazy. Some guys were spraying their hair pink and green. Others were painting their faces.

The boys were putting on their witch outfits when Zak said, "Okay, A.J., where're the signs?"

A.J. froze. The signs! "Oh, no," he said. "They're in my backpack in the classroom!"

"Not cool," said Mike.

"Better sneak back and get 'em," said Tyler.

A.J. zipped up the black gown he'd borrowed

from his crazy Aunt Clara, and headed back down the stairway to the classroom.

The hallways were quiet during lunchtime. All students were either in the cafeteria or out on the playground. No one was allowed near the classrooms, and A.J. knew he'd be in big trouble if he were caught.

He tried the door handle. It was unlocked! He peered into the room. It was dark and there was no movement inside. Slowly he pulled the door open, looking around to make sure no one saw him.

He opened the heavy door quietly and stepped inside. It should only take a second to . . .

". . . and Lord, although I love these kids, You know I don't love the way they act on Halloween."

It was Mrs. Todd. She was praying! A.J. ducked behind a coat hanging on the coat rack. He was lucky she hadn't heard him, but how could he get out of there now?

"Teaching is just such a hard job sometimes, God," Mrs. Todd continued. "Some of these kids have such a tough life. It's a wonder they can learn at all."

Anthony listened quietly as she prayed for each child.

God? What do I do now? Mrs. Todd is praying for us. She just prayed for me—that I do well in class and not let my friends get me in trouble.

Maybe I was wrong about her. . . . She really seems to care about us, about me. I guess a teacher would have to be nuts to do this job if she didn't like kids.

Okay, Lord, I guess this teacher trick thing was pretty stupid. Somehow I'll have to tell the guys the deal is off.

"But please just help us all get through the day. And let me be an example of Your light. Thank You, Father. Amen."

A.J. was creeping toward the door when he heard, "Hello there. Who is that? Anthony?"

"Uh, yes, ma'am," he said, turning around. "I, uh, just forgot part of our, I mean my, costume. I've got it now, so I'll just be . . ."

"So you heard me praying?" Mrs. Todd asked.

"Yeah, Mrs. Todd," A.J. said, "I'm real sorry . . . about a lot of things. But you've helped me out now, and I'll just be going."

"Okay," said Mrs. Todd, getting up from her chair. "And by the way, Anthony?"

"Yes," said A.J.

"For Halloween?" she said, pausing.

"Yes, ma'am?"

Mrs. Todd smiled a glowing kind of smile, the kind that comes from inside and spills over everywhere. "For Halloween, Anthony . . . be a light to the world, okay? You know what I mean?"

Anthony smiled back, the same kind of smile. "Yeah, I do, Mrs. Todd. Cool idea—a light. Triple dip cool idea."

Sharing the Faith

Just outside the boys' bathroom, A.J. prayed.

God, I don't have a clue of what I'm going to tell the guys. Help me, please.

He breathed in deeply, then pulled the door open. "Okay, here's the deal," he said.

Zak, Mike, and Tyler stood just inside, fully dressed in black, arms linked together, faces painted green and white. One had on a mask that looked like a giant wart.

"Hey," said the wart face, "get the signs?"

"No signs, guys," said A.J. "I went back to the classroom and found Mrs. Todd, uh, praying."

"Praying?" said Zak. "In school? Isn't that illegal? I'm going to tell . . ."

"Cool it, Zak," said A.J. "She wasn't praying *with* us. She was praying *for* us. I decided that's something I need to do more of too."

"Pray?" asked Mike. "You pray?"

"Yeah," said A.J. "I'm a Christian. And praying is just talking with the coolest guy you could ever meet—God."

"Yeah?" asked Tyler. "Do you hear stuff back?"

"Well, sort of," said A.J. "He reminds me of things I've read in the Bible."

"You read the Bible?" asked Mike. "Whoa!"

"Yeah, my dad and I do together," said A.J. "And anyway, when I heard Mrs. Todd praying, I thought about something."

"Yeah?" asked Zak, looking interested.

"Well," said A.J., "I think God has made Mrs. Todd my—our—teacher this year. And maybe I was just looking at things the wrong way."

The boys stood there staring at A.J. He took off his costume and stuffed it into his backpack.

"A.J.?" said Mike.

"Yeah?" said A.J.

"You're weird," said Mike, rubbing his eyes and smearing the white gunk all around.

"Double weird," said Tyler.

"Triple weird," said Zak.

"Triple dip weird," all three chimed.

"Thanks, guys," said A.J., pushing open the bathroom door. "Hope you're all as weird as I am some day. And by the way, Zak. I hope you didn't mail that letter."

"Nah," said Zak. "I lost it."

A.J. left the three standing there, staring blankly. They thought they knew him. But somehow as he bounced down the stairs, he looked different to them. He had on his regular clothes—jeans, sweatshirt, hightop shoes. But there was definitely something different.

Down the eighty-four steps to the playground, A.J. found Emily sitting alone under a pine tree. She was studying for their spelling test.

"Hey, Emmo," said A.J.

"Hey, Dummo," said Emily, not looking up.

"Would you quiz me on the words once or twice?" he asked.

"Are you sick or something?" Emily asked.

"Why?" asked A.J.

"Well, first you want to study your spelling," said Emily. "Second, you want to study with me, your sister."

46

She paused, looking at him for the first time. "And third, where is your costume? I heard you and the guys were going to dress like witches and make fun of Mrs. Todd."

"Nah," said A.J. "I changed my mind about that. Or I should say, God changed my mind."

"God did?" she asked.

"Yeah, God did," said A.J.

Emily stared at her brother. He didn't usually talk about God stuff with her. In fact, this was probably the first time he had.

He stood there shuffling his feet and trying to hold back a smile—a glowing kind of smile. In fact, Emily thought he looked like he does when he's just had five pieces of pepperoni pizza.

"Respect," said Emily.

"Right," said A.J. "I learned that adults, especially Mrs. Todd, aren't so bad, and they deserve my respect."

"No, Dummo," said Emily. "Respect—spell it! It's on our test today."

"Duh," said A.J., hitting his head.

The twins practiced their words for about ten minutes. Then the bell rang and they headed for the lineup. Students were chattering more than usual. Marc from Mrs. Bender's class had confessed to pulling the fire alarm. He was suspended, but the parade and party were now a go.

Things are looking up, thought A.J. as they walked to class. Mrs. Todd turned out to be a human being after all. If he passed his spelling test, his folks said he could go to the soccer tournament Saturday. And now they were going to have cupcakes instead of writing time.

Back in the room, A.J. and Emily looked at all their friends who were sitting in the wrong places. The twins looked at each other and smiled. Somehow they didn't seem to fit in. Yes, in the midst of the monsters and clowns, A.J. and Emily were definitely triple dip weird.